HENRIETTA AND
THE GHOST CHASE

Starring Henrietta:

HENRIETTA AND THE GHOST CHASE

Stan Cullimore
Illustrated by John Farman

YOUNG CORGI BOOKS

HENRIETTA AND THE GHOST CHASE

A YOUNG CORGI BOOK 0 552 52747 5

First published in Great Britain by Piccadilly Press Ltd.

PRINTING HISTORY
Piccadilly Press edition published 1992
Young Corgi edition published 1994

Text copyright © Stan Cullimore, 1992
Illustrations copyright © John Farman, 1992

Young Corgi Books are published by Transworld Publishers Ltd.,
61–63 Uxbridge Road, Ealing, London W5 5SA, in Australia by
Transworld Publishers (Australia) Pty. Ltd., 15–25 Helles Avenue,
Moorebank, NSW 2170, and in New Zealand by Transworld
Publishers (N.Z.) Ltd., 3 William Pickering Drive, Albany, Auckland.

Printed and bound in Great Britain by
Cox & Wyman Ltd., Reading, Berks.

CONTENTS

STORY ONE

ITCHING-POWDER PEPPER

"Dad," said Daniel as he washed up
the dishes after breakfast one Saturday,
"can we go to the library this morning?
I want to look at some books about
computers."

His father thought for a moment, then
nodded. "All right, we can go when I've
finished my tea. Mum won't be back from
town with Baby-Rose until this afternoon,
and I like going there."

Just then Henrietta walked into the

room holding a big blue book. "Going where?"

"To the library. Dad and I are going to the library," said Daniel, drying his hands and sensibly folding the towel on the towel rack.

"Can I come?" asked Henrietta.

Daniel snorted. "You! What do you want to go to the library for?"

Henrietta looked at the book she was carrying. It was called *The Big Blue Book of Practical Jokes*. She smiled. "There's something I want to try out."

"Well you can't come," snapped Daniel. "You ALWAYS cause trouble at the library. Dad and I are going to have a nice, quiet look at some books. We don't want you spoiling it for us!"

"Please, Dad, can I come?" begged Henrietta, smiling her sweetest smile at her father. "There's something I REALLY want to find out."

Her father took off his glasses and began to clean them with a hanky. "Of course you can come, Henrietta, we can't leave you here on your own. And I'm very glad that you WANT to go to the library." He then gave his usual lecture about how useful libraries were, especially if there was something you really wanted to find out all about.

While her father was polishing his glasses and not watching what she was doing, Henrietta went to the cupboard and got out the pepperpot.

She slid it into her pocket. She had just read in *The Big Blue Book of Practical Jokes* that if you used pepper as an itching powder it was REALLY itchy. And she wanted to find out if this was true.

When her father had finished talking and put his glasses back on again, Henrietta nodded and pretended that she had been listening. "You're right there, Dad! Libraries are very good places. Come on then, let's go."

Her father finished his tea and stood up. "All right."

Ten minutes later they were standing outside the library. Henrietta's father was just about to open the door when he suddenly stopped. "Now don't forget, Henrietta, when we get inside you MUST behave yourself. No running around pretending to be an aeroplane, like you did last time."

Henrietta nodded. "Of course not,

Dad!" She covered her mouth so her father wouldn't see her grinning.

"No climbing up the bookshelves, like you did the time before."

Henrietta tried not to giggle and failed. "Hehehe!" But she managed to make it sound as if she was coughing, so her father wouldn't notice.

"And definitely NO shouting, or banging or making loud noises, like you did the time before that. People who come to the library want peace and quiet. Do I make myself clear?"

Henrietta stopped giggling and tried to look serious.

"And if you do behave yourself, I might just buy you an ice-cream when we come out."

"Thanks, Dad," shouted Henrietta. "But what about Daniel?"

Daniel squawked. "I always behave myself in the library."

Dad nodded. "You're right, Daniel, you do. But I have to be fair. As long as you BOTH behave yourselves, I'll buy you BOTH an ice-cream. All right Henrietta?"

Henrietta nodded.

"It's not fair. I ALWAYS behave myself in the library," grumbled Daniel. "I'm always very sensible and very quiet, not like Henrietta."

Henrietta stroked the pepperpot in her pocket and smiled. "We'll soon see about that, won't we."

Once they got inside, Daniel quickly found a book on computers and started reading through it, to see if he wanted to take it home.

"Please, do sit down, Daniel dearest." Henrietta pulled out a chair and brought it over to where Daniel was standing.

"Thank you," said Daniel, not really paying attention. As he sat down

Henrietta took out the pepperpot and
sprinkled pepper down the back of his
trousers. She waited to see what would
happen next.

She didn't have to wait very long!

Almost at once Daniel began to squirm,
as the pepper started to itch. "Ooo-ooh,"
he squealed. Suddenly with a CRASH

and a BANG, he slipped off the chair and dropped the book onto the floor.

His father appeared. "Daniel, behave yourself. This isn't like you. You're making far too much noise."

"Sorry," whispered Daniel. "I think there was something wrong with that chair. It felt all itchy." He picked up his book and carried on reading.

Henrietta crept over to him and gently poured a little of the pepper down his neck, inside his shirt collar. Then she put the pepperpot back into her pocket and tiptoed off into a corner.

Daniel wriggled his shoulders. Suddenly he yelped as the pepper got to work. He threw down the book he was holding and began to dance around the room rubbing and pulling and scratching at his shirt. Henrietta quickly picked up a book and pretended to be reading it.

By now, Daniel was making so much noise that his father appeared again, frowning. "Daniel, whatever do you think you're doing? You won't get an ice-cream if you carry on like this. Why can't you be more like Henrietta. She's behaving perfectly, look at her reading to herself quietly."

Daniel slowly stopped jumping around

as the pepper fell out of his shirt onto the floor. He looked at Henrietta. She was standing quietly in a corner holding a book up to her nose.

In fact, she was trying hard not to laugh out loud. "This pepper makes FANTASTIC itching powder," she chuckled.

Suddenly she grinned. She had just thought of a brilliant idea. She got some of the pepper, put it onto her hanky and walked over to Daniel.

"Quick," she hissed. "Blow your nose, it's starting to run." She gave him her hanky.

"Thanks, Henrietta," whispered Daniel. He blew his nose and put the hanky in his pocket. Henrietta covered her ears and waited for the pepper to begin its work. She didn't have to wait long. Daniel's nose began to itch, and itch, and ITCH.

"Ah . . . ah . . . ATISHOO!" sneezed Daniel.

Henrietta giggled. "Now I'm not the only one with a hyper-sneeze. Hehehe."

Her father reappeared. "Right, come on. We're leaving. Put that book back, Daniel – there'll be no ice-cream for you, young man. You're a disgrace, I've never heard so much noise in all my life."

Five minutes later they were sitting in the café next door to the library. In front of Henrietta was an enormous bowl full of chocolate and banana ice-cream.

Daniel sat opposite her, with his mouth wide open, staring at the bowl.

His father shook his head. "I've never known you behave so badly in the library before, Daniel. Whatever is the matter with you?"

Daniel didn't reply, he was too busy staring at the ice-cream.

"I'm so clever," thought Henrietta

happily. "It wasn't Daniel who behaved badly, it was ME. But Dad doesn't know that, so I get an enormous ice-cream and Daniel gets NOTHING! I'm so glad I

came to the library – I must come again." She bent down to pick up her spoon and accidentally dipped her nose in banana ice-cream. "Where has my hanky got to," she muttered, emptying out her pockets.

"Here it is," replied Daniel, passing it to her.

Henrietta snatched it and wiped the ice-cream from her nose. Suddenly she noticed some of the pepper she had sprinkled on the hanky falling onto her ice-cream. "Oh no. Itching-powder pepper on my ice, ah . . . ice, ah . . . . ATISHOO!"

She did a Henrietta hyper-sneeze that blew all the chocolate and banana ice-cream out of the bowl, across the table and right . . . into Daniel's open mouth.

"Ratburgers," groaned Henrietta. "Daniel's got all my ice-cream and I've got nothing." Daniel's face went bright red. "There again," chuckled Henrietta, "maybe ice-cream doesn't taste very nice when it's got itching-powder pepper on it! Hehehe."

14

STORY TWO

HAPPY BIRTHDAY, HENRIETTA

One evening Henrietta's mother looked at the clock, put down her knitting and folded her arms.

"Right, Henrietta. Time for bed."

Henrietta was sitting on the sofa. She was licking her lips and thinking about tomorrow.

Tomorrow was her birthday.

As far as Henrietta was concerned, the best thing about birthdays was definitely, BIRTHDAY CAKE. Her mother

ALWAYS made her an enormous birthday cake, covered in green icing. Henrietta felt hungry just thinking about it!

"Did you hear me, Henrietta. It's time for bed."

Henrietta jumped. "What did you say, Mum?"

"It's bedtime," said her mother.

Henrietta smiled sweetly. "OK. You go to bed then if you want to, Mum, I'm not tired yet."

Her mother sighed. "It's not MY bedtime, Henrietta, it's YOURS, whether you're tired or not. You haven't forgotten what day it is tomorrow have you?"

Henrietta grinned. "Of course not." Suddenly she snapped her fingers. "I know what it is. You want me out of the way so that you can get the cake ready for tomorrow, don't you!" She began dancing around the room with excitement.

Her mother nodded. "That's right. The cake for you and Baby-Rose."

Henrietta stopped dancing. "WHAT!" She sat down. "Why are you making a cake for me AND Baby-Rose, Mum?"

Her mother shook her head. "You haven't forgotten, have you Henrietta? Tomorrow is your birthday and . . ."

Henrietta started dancing around the room again, singing loudly "Happy

birthday to me, Happy birthday to me!"

"Calm down, Henrietta, or you'll wake Baby-Rose up," sighed her mother, covering her ears.

Henrietta calmed down. "No need to shout, Mum, Baby-Rose is asleep!"

Her mother closed her eyes and started again.

"I was saying, that since tomorrow is your birthday AND Baby-Rose goes to nursery for the very first time, I've decided to bake one cake for you both to share. As a special treat you can have a piece for breakfast, if you like."

Henrietta gulped. "To SHARE! But I ALWAYS eat all my birthday cake on my own!"

"I know you do, Henrietta," said her mother. "And you ALWAYS end up feeling sick afterwards as well."

"No I don't!"

"Yes you do," said her mother. "So

tomorrow you can share it. Three-quarters for you, and one-quarter for Baby-Rose. Now run along and clean your teeth and stop being so silly. It's time for bed."

Henrietta slowly walked out of the room and went upstairs.

As she stood in front of the bathroom mirror, brushing her teeth, the smell of freshly baked cake floated up from the kitchen. Henrietta put down her toothbrush and pulled an unhappy face.

"It's not fair, I never EVER share my birthday cake. And I don't ALWAYS feel sick, just sometimes!" She wiped her mouth with her sleeve and walked sadly into her room.

She got changed into her pyjamas quietly. Suddenly, she smiled. She had just thought of a brilliant idea.

"Mum said we had to have one-quarter for Baby-Rose and three-quarters for me.

But she DIDN'T say that the quarters had to be the same size, did she. So I'll just have to make sure that my quarters are the BIGGEST!"

With that, she climbed into bed and turned off the light.

Downstairs in the kitchen, Mum was carefully putting green icing on an enormous cake.

"Do you know what?" she said. "I felt awful seeing Henrietta's face when I told her I wasn't making her a cake all of her own."

Henrietta's father nodded. "She did look upset, didn't she?"

Henrietta's mother put down the spoon she was holding. "There, I've finished." She smiled. "And I've just had a marvellous idea! Why don't I make Baby-Rose a little cake all of her own, so Henrietta doesn't have to share her birthday cake. As long as we can stop Henrietta from stuffing it all down in one go, she'll be all right."

She picked up the cake and carried it over to the table.

Henrietta's father smiled. "I can't wait to see Henrietta's face when she finds out she DOESN'T have to share her cake. She'll be so glad she might even remember to say thank you!"

An hour later there were TWO cakes sitting on the table, one big and one small.

The big one, for Henrietta, was covered with green icing.

The small one, for Baby-Rose, was coated in thick milk chocolate with jelly-babies on top.

"Now we really HAVE finished," said Henrietta's mother. "The question is, where shall we put Henrietta's? We must make SURE that she doesn't find it and eat it all before we can stop her."

She looked around the kitchen.

"On the top shelf?" suggested Henrietta's father. "Henrietta would never think of looking there." He picked up the enormous cake and placed it carefully on the top shelf out of sight.

Henrietta's mother then picked up the small cake from the table and put it in the cupboard under the sink.

The next morning, before anyone else was awake, Henrietta sat up in bed. She rubbed her eyes and yawned, then she looked at the clock.

"Good, I've got plenty of time to go and look for this cake I've got to share with Baby-Rose. Mum and Dad won't be up for ages." She quickly got dressed and tiptoed downstairs to the kitchen.

"Now where does Mum usually put her

cakes," she muttered. She thought for a moment. "I know!" She opened the cupboard under the sink and looked in.

There, in front of her eyes, was a small cake covered in thick milk chocolate with jelly-babies on top.

Henrietta picked it up and took a bite. "Hmm," she sighed. Just as she was about to take another, she heard footsteps. It was her father coming to make a cup of tea for her mother.

"Ratburgers! I mustn't let Dad see me," thought Henrietta. Quickly she jumped into the cupboard and closed the door behind her.

She took another bite of the cake. Then another.

Her father finished making the tea and looked around for the tray to take it upstairs.

"Where have I put it?" he muttered. He bent down. "I know where it is. It's in the cupboard under the sink."

He opened the cupboard door, and almost fell as he jumped back in amazement.

"What on earth are you doing in THERE, Henrietta?" he exclaimed.

Henrietta burped. "I'm sharing my cake with Baby-Rose. This is her piece." She held up all that was left.

Half a jelly-baby.

"And I don't feel sick, ONE LITTLE BIT!"

Her father shook his head. "I don't believe it, Henrietta. How could you do such a thing?"

Henrietta climbed out of the cupboard and looked puzzled. "What do you mean – do you think I've left her too much?"

Her father sighed. "No, I don't." He softened slightly. "Do you realise, Henrietta, that little cake you've just scoffed was for Baby-Rose. Mum made

TWO cakes last night, one for each of you. Because we felt sorry for you having to share your birthday cake. We realised that you were counting on the whole cake for yourself."

Henrietta blinked and rubbed her tummy sadly, then she put her arms around her father's waist. "I've been greedy, haven't I, Daddy?"

Her father nodded, realising that she was trying to get round him. Suddenly he smiled and stroked her head. "It is your birthday after all, so I'm not going to tell you off. But don't ever do anything like that again, Henrietta. Greed is not a pretty sight, particularly in little girls!"

He reached up and got the enormous cake down from the top shelf. "See what it says: HAPPY BIRTHDAY, HENRIETTA! Shall I cut you a piece – what's wrong, Henrietta?"

Henrietta looked as if she was about to cry.

Her father patted her on the head. "I told you, no-one's going to tell you off for being greedy on your birthday."

"It's not that," groaned Henrietta.

"Well, what IS wrong with you?"

Henrietta pulled a face.

"I FEEL SICK!"

STORY THREE

GHOST CHASE

"I'm bored," moaned Henrietta as she dropped her green banana skin behind the sofa. "I hate Sunday afternoons. There's never anything to do."

Her mum put down the iron she was holding and scowled. "Nothing to do! I've been slaving away all day! Why, you could certainly help me, Henrietta, I've got plenty to do."

"Like what?" asked Henrietta, picking up another green banana.

"Like putting down that banana and taking all those clean sheets upstairs to the cupboard in Daniel's room."

Henrietta was just about to say, "No thanks, Mum. That sounds REALLY boring," when she saw the look on her mother's face. So she smiled sweetly instead. She didn't want to lose any of her pocket money like she had last week!

"OK Mum. Whereabouts in the cupboard do the sheets go?"

"On the bottom shelf."

Henrietta put the green banana in her pocket, picked up the pile of clean white sheets and ran upstairs. When she got to the landing, she stopped to get her breath back. She was lucky and she knew it! Usually when her mother went on like that, Henrietta had to be helpful for the rest of the day.

Henrietta smiled. She had just thought of a brilliant idea; she would go into

Daniel's room without knocking. He always hated that!

She opened the door to her sensible brother's room and marched in.

"Get out!" Daniel shouted, not looking up from his computer. He knew Henrietta's heavy step.

"Why should I?" Henrietta opened the cupboard door and threw the clean sheets onto the bottom shelf.

"Because you should have knocked first. I'm busy."

Henrietta smiled her very sweetest smile. "But I'm helping Mum." She went and stood behind her brother and watched what he was doing. "Is that your new game, *Ghost Chase*?"

Daniel nodded, "Yeah. It's brilliant. You have to catch all the ghosts. I only need to get one more and I've won."

"Can I have a go?" asked Henrietta.

Daniel smiled. "You!" He laughed.

"You wouldn't have a clue how to play
Ghost Chase!"

"Yes I would."

"Wouldn't!"

"Would," shouted Henrietta.

"Wouldn't," yelled Daniel.

Mum stuck her head round the door.
"Stop shouting, you two. You'll wake
Baby-Rose. If you've got nothing to do,

you can always come and help me.
There's lots to be done." She closed the
door and went downstairs.

"That was your fault," hissed Daniel,
going back to his game.

Henrietta stuck out her tongue and
pulled a face. "Creep!" Suddenly she had
an idea. She leant forward and stared at
the computer. Daniel was about to catch
the last ghost and win the game. "Daniel,
what happens if I press that red button?"

"Which red button?" asked Daniel.

Henrietta took a deep breath. "This
one!" She pressed the large red button
labelled STOP. With a buzz and a whirr
the computer switched itself off. The
Ghost Chase game disappeared from the
screen.

"You did that on purpose!" squealed
Daniel, stamping his foot. "I was just
about to win as well." He stood up. "I'm
going to tell Mum." He stomped out of

the room and slammed the door behind him.

"Double creep," shouted Henrietta. She sighed happily. "I do love annoying Daniel." She got the green banana out of her pocket and began munching it.

Downstairs in the kitchen Mum was trying not to get annoyed. "Daniel, do you have to come crashing down those stairs like an elephant wearing hobnailed boots? You'll wake Baby-Rose up."

"It's not my fault. It's Henrietta. She started it. She came into my room without knocking."

Mum sighed. "So you wouldn't let her play your new game. I know. I heard it all from down here."

"Henrietta wouldn't have a clue how to play *Ghost Chase*," grumbled Daniel. "She's too stupid."

"Daniel, don't say such things about your sister!" Mum sat down. "I know

Henrietta can be a little bit annoying sometimes."

Daniel snorted. "More like all the time!"

Mum sighed. "But it would be nice if you could let her have a little go on your computer. You know she loves playing with it. Look, I'm going to have a nice hot cup of tea. Why don't you run along and let your sister have a go at your new game?"

"All right Mum, if you say so," sighed Daniel. He was terribly sensible sometimes. Then he turned and went, quietly, up to his room. "That pesky Henrietta, she'll be useless at *Ghost Chase*. I know she will," he muttered.

Upstairs, Henrietta was sitting in front of Daniel's computer trying to work out how to switch it on. When she heard Daniel coming back she jumped up. "If Daniel catches me here, there'll be trouble. I'd better hide." She threw her green banana skin onto the floor and crawled into the cupboard where she hid amongst the pile of clean white sheets she had put there earlier.

Daniel walked into the room and smiled. Henrietta had disappeared; now he wouldn't have to let her have a go on his game. He noticed the open cupboard and frowned. She hadn't bothered to close the cupboard door after she had put the sheets away! He tutted to himself and clicked the door shut. Then he sat down at his computer.

"Now, where was I?" He thought for a moment. Then he rubbed his hands together and smiled. *"Ghost Chase!"* He switched on the computer and got ready to play another game.

In the cupboard, Henrietta was beginning to get a bit hot and bothered. It was very dark with the door closed. And somehow she had got all twisted up inside one of the sheets. To make matters worse, her nose was beginning to itch.

"Ratburgers! Why did that Daniel have to close the door. He's such a stupid, ah . . . stupid, ah . . . Oh no! Not my sneezy nose." She tried to stop it. But it was too late. "ATISHOO." She did a Henrietta hyper-sneeze that blew her and all the clean white sheets right out of the cupboard.

"HELP," cried Henrietta. She tried to stand up but her foot slipped on the green banana skin that she had dropped.

"Woooo . . . oooh," moaned Henrietta as she began to slide across the room.

Daniel turned at the sound of the sneeze and saw all the sheets flying out of the cupboard. He gulped. Then he heard

a groaning sound and saw what looked like an enormous cloud of white smoke rushing towards him.

In fact it was Henrietta. She was all wrapped up in a sheet and had just stepped on the green banana skin. The sound he heard was Henrietta moaning as she slid across the floor. But Daniel didn't know that! He leapt up and nearly knocked over his chair . . .

"GHOSTS! They're after me. HELP! They've come to chase me away." He turned and ran out of the door, still shouting at the top of his voice that the ghosts were after him.

At that moment Henrietta stopped sliding. She took off the sheet that had been covering her and looked slowly all around the room. She chuckled. "Now that's what I call a REAL game of *Ghost Chase*! Imagine Daniel thinking I was a proper ghost."

She grinned happily to herself and pulled the sheet back over her head. This was the best game she had played for a long time! The question was, who could she go and *Ghost Chase* next? If only she could find someone who would scream, that would be BRILLIANT. But who?

Five minutes later the house was filled by the sound of Baby-Rose squealing. Her mother picked her up. "What's the matter, Baby-Rose? Anyone would think that you've just been chased by a ghost or something!"

Now who would do a thing like that?

STORY FOUR

CHESS

"Henrietta, do you want to learn how to play chess?" asked Henrietta's father.

"No thanks, Dad. Chess is boring," yawned Henrietta. She was lying on the sofa watching television.

Her sensible brother Daniel snorted. "Boring! Chess isn't half as boring as watching stupid quiz shows on television all day!" Before Henrietta could reply her mother walked into the room, strode over to the television and switched it off.

"I've just been into your bedrooms, Daniel and Henrietta. They are both a disgrace. I want you to go and tidy them up RIGHT away. Go on, off you go!"

Daniel stood up sadly and smiled his most sensible smile. "All right, Mum, if you say so. But Dad was just going to teach me how to play chess. Now he'll probably go and do something else and I'll never learn how to play."

His father and mother exchanged glances.

"OK then, YOU can tidy your room later, Daniel," said Mum, "after you have finished playing with Dad."

Daniel hugged his mother. "Thanks, Mum. I will do it later, I promise." He stuck out his tongue out as he passed Henrietta.

On the sofa, Henrietta looked as if she was going to be sick. "What a creep!" she groaned.

Her mother turned round. "Did you say something, Henrietta?" Henrietta shook her head. "Then perhaps you should go upstairs and start tidying your room."

Henrietta jumped to her feet. "I can't."

Her mother frowned. "Why can't you?"

"Because Dad said that he was going to teach ME how to play chess too."

Her father burst out laughing. "I thought you said that chess was boring."

Henrietta smiled sweetly. "I did. But it's not as boring as tidying your room!"

Her father winked at her mother. "Go on, let her off."

Her mother shook her head.

"I don't know who's worse sometimes, you or your father." She sighed. "All right then. YOU can tidy your room later as well, Henrietta. But I warn you both, they'd better be tidied up before you go to bed." With that she went upstairs to get Baby-Rose up for her supper.

Half an hour later, Dad stood up and stretched. "There you are. Now you both know how all the different pieces move, you're ready to play a game. I'll watch, and help you when you don't know what to do."

"How do you WIN at chess?" asked Daniel.

His father thought for a moment. "Well, there are lots of ways. But the easiest way to do it, is to get nearly all the other person's pieces off the board. Then you've won!"

At that moment Baby-Rose crawled into the room. She sat on the rug and burst out crying. Dad bent down and picked her up. "What's the matter?" he said gently. Baby-Rose began to cry even louder.

"Look," said Dad, "I've got an idea.
Why don't you two start playing, while I
go and give Baby-Rose a drink. I think
she might be thirsty. I won't be long."

When he had gone Daniel and
Henrietta started to play their first ever
REAL game of chess.

"This is really EXCITING, isn't it,
Henrietta," said Daniel.

Henrietta yawned. "No, it isn't. It's
really BORING." She grinned. "But it's

better than tidying up my room."

Daniel moved one of his pieces and took one of Henrietta's off the board. "Look, I've just taken one of your pawns."

Henrietta yawned again. "How really exciting!" She moved one of her pieces.

"I don't mind tidying up my room. I hate it being messy anyway," said Daniel. He smiled his most sensible smile, AGAIN!

"Then why don't you tidy up MY room as well as yours?" suggested Henrietta. "I wouldn't mind." Suddenly she sat up. She had just thought of a brilliant idea. "Hey Daniel. Why don't we make it that whoever loses this game of chess has to tidy up BOTH of our rooms."

Daniel frowned. "All right Henrietta, if you want to. But you're losing at the moment. I've taken three of your pieces off the board already. At this rate, you'll be tidying up your room AND mine!"

"Oh no I won't," thought Henrietta with a chuckle. "I've got a plan!"

Suddenly she coughed. "I'm thirsty. Shall we go through to the kitchen and get a drink?"

Daniel nodded. "All right." He stood up as Henrietta crouched down and began to play with her shoelace. "What are you doing, Henrietta?"

"Just tying up my lace, it's come loose. You go on ahead. I'll meet you in the kitchen."

"Your lace looks fine to me!" said Daniel as he strolled out of the room.

When he had gone Henrietta jumped up. "For someone who is supposed to be so sensible and so clever, my brother certainly is STUPID! Now to carry out the next stage of my clever plan."

She went over to the chessboard and picked up some of Daniel's pieces. But before she could hide them, she heard footsteps in the hall. Daniel was coming back. Quickly she pushed them up her sleeve and out of sight.

"Here you are. You took so long that I decided to bring your drink for you," said Daniel.

Henrietta didn't reply. She was too busy trying to stop Daniel's pieces from falling back down her sleeve. Daniel sat down and looked at the chessboard.

He frowned.

"That's funny. Some of my pieces are missing, they must have fallen onto the floor." He looked underneath the table. "They aren't down there. Where can they have got to?"

At that moment, Dad walked in, still carrying Baby-Rose. He came over to the table.

"How are you two getting on then?" He whistled. "It looks to me as if Henrietta is going to win this game, Daniel. You've hardly got any pieces left on the board!"

Daniel scratched his head. "I don't know where the rest of them have got to. They were here when I went to get a drink and left Henrietta tying up her shoelace."

Slowly, both Dad and Daniel turned to Henrietta.

"Do you know where Daniel's pieces

are, Henrietta?" asked Dad.

Henrietta gulped and licked her lips. Then her nose went bright red, as it always did when she was caught out.

Daniel narrowed his eyes. "I bet she does. Whoever loses this game has to tidy up BOTH of our rooms. I expect she only wanted me to go to the kitchen to get a drink, so that SHE could hide some of my pieces. Then I would lose the game and tidy up HER room as well as MINE."

"What an AWFUL thing to say," said Henrietta. "I would never do anything like that, would I, Baby-Rose?" She turned to Baby-Rose and tickled her chin, hoping that Daniel and her father would forget all about the missing chess pieces.

Baby-Rose laughed happily and tugged at Henrietta's sleeve.

"No, Baby-Rose," whispered Henrietta. "Don't do that!" But it was too late. With a **PING** and a **PONG** and a **WALLOP**, all of Daniel's pieces fell out of her sleeve and onto the floor.

"I think," said Henrietta quietly, "I'll just go and tidy my room."

"Oh, Henrietta," whispered Daniel with a smug grin, "**DON'T FORGET TO TIDY MINE, AS WELL!**"

HENRIETTA AND THE TOOTH FAIRY

by Stan Cullimore

Illustrated by John Farman

"Oh no. Not my sneezy nose." Henrietta tried to stop it. But it was too late . . .

Henrietta is always being naughty. She doesn't *want* to be like her sensible brother Daniel. And her sneezy nose keeps making her sneeze at all the wrong moments – at the swimming pool, buying new shoes, or trying to do good deeds. When Henrietta gets a wobbly tooth, she wants it to fall out quickly so that the tooth fairy will come. But things don't work out quite as Henrietta plans . . .

A delightful series of four stories about the mischievous Henrietta and her family – ideal for beginner readers.

'Children responded well to this lively, active book which has plenty of drawings to sustain their interest' *Federation of Children's Book Groups, Pick of the Year*

0 552 52745 9

YOUNG CORGI

HENRIETTA'S BUBBLE TROUBLE

by Stan Cullimore

Illustrated by John Farman

Upstairs in the bath Henrietta was covered all over in soft frothy bubbles. So was the floor.

"Yippee," she cried, as she pushed her rubber duck under the water. "I love bubbles."

Henrietta and her sensible brother, Daniel are being given a real treat but first she must have a bath without making any mess. That's not easy to do when you're Henrietta! Once again her sneezy nose looks as if it will land her in trouble, or will it?

Another lively collection of four stories about the mischievous Henrietta and her family – ideal for beginner readers.

0 552 52746 7

YOUNG
CORGI

A SELECTED LIST OF TITLES AVAILABLE
FROM YOUNG CORGI BOOKS

THE PRICES SHOWN BELOW WERE CORRECT AT THE TIME OF GOING TO PRESS. HOWEVER TRANSWORLD PUBLISHERS RESERVE THE RIGHT TO SHOW NEW RETAIL PRICES ON COVERS WHICH MAY DIFFER FROM THOSE PREVIOUSLY ADVERTISED IN THE TEXT OR ELSEWHERE.

☐	52450 6	**Your Guess Is As Good As Mine**	*Bernard Ashley*	£1.75
☐	52662 2	**The Big Hit**	*Rob Childs*	£2.50
☐	52746 7	**Henrietta's Bubble Trouble**	*Stan Cullimore*	£2.50
☐	52745 9	**Henrietta and the Tooth Fairy**	*Stan Cullimore*	£2.50
☐	52301 1	**T.R. Bear: Enter T.R.**	*Terrance Dicks*	£2.50
☐	52700 9	**T.R. Bear: T.R. at the Zoo**	*Terrance Dicks*	£1.75
☐	52559 6	**The Magic Camera**	*Adèle Geras*	£1.99
☐	52497 2	**Jason and the School Bully**	*Eric Johns*	£2.50
☐	52614 2	**The Three Bears Lend a Hand**	*Eric Johns*	£2.50
☐	52516 2	**Ursula Climbing**	*Sheila Lavelle*	£1.75
☐	52558 8	**The Scary Mouse**	*Marjorie Newman*	£2.50
☐	52621 5	**The Grand Bristleton Easter Egg**	*Ann Ruffell*	£1.99
☐	52415 8	**My Gang**	*Catherine Sefton*	£1.75
☐	52545 6	**Purr**	*Jennifer Zabel*	£2.50

All Young Corgi Books are available at your bookshop or newsagent, or can be ordered from the following address:

Transworld Publishers Ltd,
Cash Sales Department,
P.O. Box 11, Falmouth, Cornwall TR10 9EN

Please send a cheque or postal order (no currency) and allow £1.00 for postage and packing for one book, an additional 50p for a second book, and an additional 30p for each subsequent book ordered to a maximum charge of £3.00 if ordering seven or more books.

Overseas customers, including Eire, please allow £2.00 for postage and packing for the first book, an additional £1.00 for a second book, and an additional 50p for each subsequent title ordered.

NAME (Block Letters) ....

ADDRESS ....

....

We hope you enjoyed reading this book. If you would like to receive details of the latest new children's books published by Transworld Publishers, please send your name and address to: The Children's Books Editor, Transworld Publishers Ltd, 61–63 Uxbridge Road, Ealing, London W5 5SA, marking your envelope CHILDREN'S NEWSLETTER.